Ian Wakes Up

written by
Pat Birt

Illustrated by
Robbie Birt

AuthorHouse™
1663 Liberty Drive
Bloomington, IN 47403
www.authorhouse.com
Phone: 1-800-839-8640

First published by AuthorHouse 8/20/2009

ISBN: 978-1-4490-1213-7 (sc)

Library of Congress Control Number: 2009908609

Printed in the United States of America
Bloomington, Indiana

This book is printed on acid-free paper.

authorHOUSE®

To   Ethan.

From Pat. Birt

Hope
you
enjoy Ethan
Rob Birt

Dear Ethan —
This was a surprise
to me! Pat & her son, Rob
live in my cul-de-sac - I
didn't know they had written
+ illustrated a book together!
They did a signing at the Used Book
Emporium where I trade in books.
Enjoy, GAC

The alarm clock made a really loud sound.

The pillow is soft and warm.

His bed is nice and cozy.

Ian opened one eye and stared at the clock.

He rolled over.

The alarm clock
would not let
him sleep.

It was time to get up!

Ian yawned
and stretched.

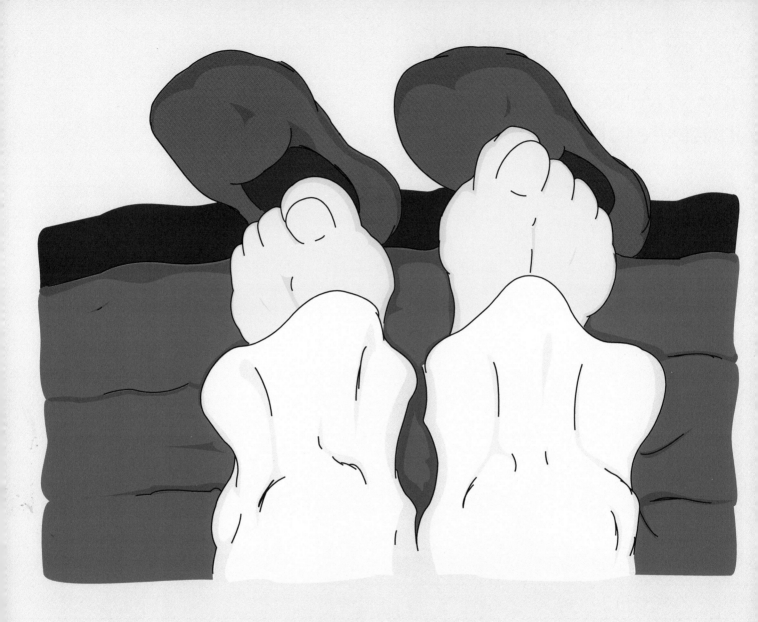

Ian hung his feet over the bed.

He looked down at his slippers.

He slowly put his
right slipper on

and then the left slipper.

Ian walked to the bathroom.

He washed his hands and face.

He went to the kitchen.

Breakfast was waiting.

It smelled so good.

Mmmm!
Pancakes and orange juice.

Breakfast was so good.

It was time for
Ian to get ready.

He had many things to do.

Ian ran off
to his room.

Threw off his P.J.'s

Ian quickly put on his clothes.

First his underwear.

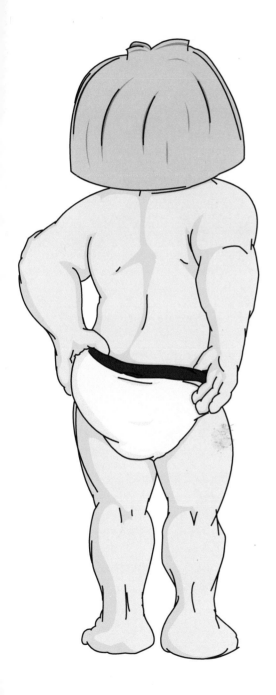

Second his pants.

Third his shirt.

Fourth his socks.

Last his shoes.

He ran out the door. Oops!

He forgot to comb his hair and brush his teeth.

Back to
the bathroom
he went.

He combed
his hair and
brushed his
teeth.

Now Ian was ready for the day.

LaVergne, TN USA
19 November 2009
164656LV00004B